This book belongs to:

Isla

Sometimes Mimi and her friends fly all the way to our huge
world and have lots of fun tiptoeing into toyshops and playing
hide-and-seek in the dolls' houses. Before they fly home again,
they whisper their stories to Clare and Cally,
so now YOU can hear them too!

For Sian: May all your magic wishes come true – Love C.B.
For Sooz, with love xx – C.J-I.

Hazel   Rose   Mimi   Acorn   Lily

First published 2015 by Macmillan Children's Books
an imprint of Pan Macmillan,
a division of Macmillan Publishers Limited
20 New Wharf Road, London N1 9RR
Associated companies throughout the world

www.panmacmillan.com

ISBN: 978-1-4472-7701-9
Text copyright © Clare Bevan 2015
Illustrations copyright © Cally Johnson-Isaacs 2015

3 5 7 9 8 6 4 2

A CIP catalogue record for this book is available from the British Library.

Printed in China

mimi's magical Fairy Friends

Catkin the Fairy Kitten

by Clare Bevan and Cally Johnson-Isaacs

MACMILLAN CHILDREN'S BOOKS

WHOOSH! Who was that whirling across the garden?

It was Mimi and her friends. They were on their way to Miss Flap's Fairy School in the Old Tree House.

"Hurry-scurry!" called Mimi. "Today Miss Flap
is going to teach us some springtime magic!"

The sky was grey and gloomy when they reached fairy school.
"Rain is on the way," said Miss Flap, "so we need to paint a rainbow!"
She picked up her box of sky colours and peeped inside.

"Oh dear!" she cried. "All my rainbow paintbrushes have vanished!"

"Don't worry, Miss Flap," said Mimi. "We'll soon find them for you — and I'm sure my fairy pet can help us." She closed her eyes and thought of a wish . . .

"Bring me my kitten,
bouncy and new —
And *let the sunshine
sparkle too!*"

POP! SPARKLE! PURR!

Catkin the fairy kitten
whizzed over their heads.

"Meow!" he mewed at Mimi.
"Hello Catkin," she smiled.
"You look wide awake today!"

Miss Flap smiled and said a rhyme to help the fairies remember the rainbow colours . . .

"Red brush, orange brush,
yellow, green and blue.
Indigo and one to go,
then violet comes too."

Away the friends flew to find the seven magic paintbrushes.

"*Red brush, orange brush,*" they sang, but Catkin was so excited he was already bouncing on a wobbly branch. A robin squawked crossly and the fairy kitten flip-flapped down again.

"Mrrrooww!" he grumbled. "Funny Catkin," laughed Mimi. "We need a red brush, not a red robin."

SQUAWK!

"I know," said Hazel, "Catkin needs a wish to help him find all the brushes." She stroked Catkin's ears and whispered . . .

"Make this wish help Catkin see
The seven brushes — speedily!"

BOING! BUZZ! MEOW! . . .

Where was Catkin now?
"I can see his tail," giggled Acorn, pointing to the door of a dusty red shed.

The fairies heard him yowl.
"Oh no!" said Lily. "Maybe he's stuck."

As fast as their wings could flap,
the fairies flew to the rescue.

To their surprise they saw Catkin playing with a red paintbrush.

"Well done Catkin!" said Lily, stroking his silky head.
"I think Hazel's wish is working!"

Now the bouncy kitten was racing round the garden pond
and gazing at a glittering goldfish.
"Don't frighten the fish, Catkin," called Mimi.
SWISH, SPLASH went his paws.
And out of the water came . . .

the orange paintbrush! "Hooray!" cheered Mimi.

Catkin mewed proudly. Then suddenly he spotted one of his favourite things — a beautiful fluttery butterfly.

He darted after it and pounced, just as the butterfly zipped away.

CRASH!

CRUNCH!

CLATTER!

Catkin landed in a heap of twigs.

"Silly Catkin!" giggled Mimi as the fairies untangled him. But he wasn't a silly kitten at all. There, hiding among the twigs, were two magic paintbrushes, sunshine yellow and leafy green.

"Thank you!" giggled the fairies.

But Catkin had gone.

"Catkin," called Mimi, "where are you?"

"I can see him," whispered Rose, pointing at a cluster of bluebells.
Two pointy ears were twitching.
"And I think we've found the blue paintbrush too," she added.

"That makes five paintbrushes!" added Hazel.
*"Red brush, orange brush,
    yellow, green and blue . . ."* she sang.
"Now we just need indigo and violet."

"What colour is indigo?" asked Acorn.
"It's a deep, dark blue," said Hazel.

The fairies looked hopefully at Catkin who was scampering after
a feather. Up the garden path twirled the feather and the kitten,
all the way to an upside-down flowerpot. And stuck in the top was . . .

"The indigo brush," laughed Rose.

Just at that moment, Miss Flap
flew down.

"Have you found all the
paintbrushes yet?" she asked.
The first drops of rain splashed down.
"We must hurry!"

The fairies looked all over, but the last brush
was nowhere to be found. As they sheltered under a tree,
Catkin's tail flicked over a small purple flower.
Soon his fur was purple too!

"Clever kitten!" Mimi laughed.
"Your tail can be the violet paintbrush!"

SPLISH, SPLOSH went the rain.
At once, the fairies grabbed the
paintbrushes and whooshed away.

High in the rainy sky, six magic paintbrushes swished . . .
and one tiny kitten tail swirled.

As the bright sun began to shine, Catkin
snuggled up to Mimi and purred happily . . .

He loved a colourful ending.

Your very own Catkin and Mimi!

Push the tab into the kitten's tummy.

Hold the fairy so her back is facing you. Squeeze her legs inwards and insert the tab marked with a star into the slot underneath her foot.

Now you have your very own fairy friends to play with!

Look out for more characters in the series!